# HARK! HARK!
# THE DOGS DO BARK

# HARK! HARK! THE DOGS DO BARK

AND OTHER RHYMES ABOUT DOGS

*Chosen by*
*Lenore Blegvad*

*Illustrated by*
*Erik Blegvad*

*A Margaret K. McElderry Book*

ATHENEUM   1976   NEW YORK

Library of Congress Cataloging in Publication Data
Main entry under title:

Hark! Hark! The dogs do bark, and other rhymes about dogs.

  "A Margaret K. McElderry book."
  SUMMARY:  A collection of both well- and lesser-known
nursery rhymes about dogs.
    1. Nursery rhymes.   2. Dogs—Juvenile poetry.
{1. Nursery rhymes.   2. Dogs—Poetry}  I. Blegvad,
Lenore.   II. Blegvad, Erik.
PZ8.3.H1997      398.8      75-9788
ISBN 0-689-50035-1

Copyright © 1975 by Erik Blegvad
All rights reserved
Published simultaneously in Canada
    by McClelland & Stewart, Ltd.
Printed photolitho in Great Britain by
Ebenezer Baylis & Son Limited
The Trinity Press, Worcester, and London
Bound by A. Horowitz & Son/Bookbinders
Clifton, New Jersey
First American Edition

The verses in this book are taken from the following sources: *The Hogarth Book of Scottish Nursery Rhymes,* collected and edited by Norah and William Montgomerie—"I've a kisty," "Roon, roon, rosie"; *The London Treasury of Nursery Rhymes,* collected by J. Murray MacBain—"Little Bingo," "There was a little dog," "The dogs of the monks," "The doggies went to the mill," "I had a little doggy"; *Mother Goose's Melodies* facsimile edition of Munroe and Francis—"Hark! Hark! The dogs do bark"; *The Nursery Rhymes of England,* collected by J. O. Halliwell—"Buff"; *The Oxford Dictionary of Nursery Rhymes,* edited by Iona and Peter Opie—"His Highness's Dog," "A Riddle," "Hey diddle, diddle"; *The Oxford Nursery Rhyme Book,* assembled by Iona and Peter Opie—"Blue Bell," "Two little dogs," "Bow, wow, wow," "Oh Where, Oh Where?," "Old 'Farmer Giles," "Old Mother Hubbard," "The little black dog"; *Trotting to Market. Poems for Infants,* chosen by Noel Holmes—"Dandy"; *National Nursery Rhymes and Nursery Songs.* Novello and Co.—"Poor Dog Bright."

# HARK! HARK! THE DOGS DO BARK

Hark! hark! the dogs do bark,
The beggars have come to town;
Some in rags, and some in tags,
And some in velvet gowns.

## BLUE BELL

I had a little dog and his name was Blue Bell,
I gave him some work, and he did it very well;
I sent him upstairs, to pick up a pin,
He stepped in the coal-scuttle up to his chin;
I sent him to the garden to pick some sage,
He tumbled down and fell in a rage;
I sent him to the cellar to draw a pot of beer,
He came up again and said there was none there.

## TWO LITTLE DOGS

Two little dogs
Sat by the fire
Over a fender of coal-dust;
Said one little dog
To the other little dog,
If you don't talk, why, I must.

## I'VE A KISTY

I've a kisty
I've a creel,
I've a baggie
Full of meal.

I've a doggie
At the door,
One, Two,
Three, Four.

(A kisty is a chest.)

## LITTLE BINGO

There was a farmer had a dog;
His name was little Bingo.
B-i-n-g-o, B-i-n-g-o, B-i-n-g-o,
And Bingo was his name, O!

Now, is that not a pretty song,
About the dog named Bingo?
B i n g o, B-i-n-g-o, B-i-n-g-o,
For Bingo was his name, O!

## BOW, WOW, WOW

Bow, wow, wow,
Whose dog art thou?
Little Tom Tinker's dog,
Bow, wow, wow.

## OH WHERE, OH WHERE?

Oh where, oh where has my little dog gone?
Oh where, oh where can he be?
With his ears cut short and his tail cut long,
Oh where, oh where is he?

## DANDY

I had a dog and his name was Dandy,
His tail was long and his legs were bandy,
His eyes were brown and his coat was sandy,
The best in the world was my dog Dandy.

## HIS HIGHNESS'S DOG

I am his Highness's dog at Kew;
Pray, tell me, sir, whose dog are you?

## THERE WAS A LITTLE DOG

There was a little dog, and he had a little tail,
And he used to wag, wag, wag it.
But whenever he was sad because he had been bad,
On the ground he would drag, drag, drag it.

He had a little nose, as of course you would suppose,
And on it was a muz-muz-muzzle,
And to get it off he'd try till a tear stood in his eye,
And he found it a puzz-puzz-puzzle.

## OLD FARMER GILES

Old Farmer Giles,
He went seven miles,
With his faithful dog, Old Rover;
And Old Farmer Giles,
When he came to the stiles,
Took a run, and jumped clean over.

## OLD MOTHER HUBBARD

Old Mother Hubbard
Went to the cupboard,
To fetch her poor dog a bone;
But when she got there
The cupboard was bare
And so the poor dog had none.

She went to the baker's
To buy him some bread;
But when she came back
The poor dog was dead.

She went to the undertaker's
To buy him a coffin;
But when she came back
The poor dog was laughing.

She took a clean dish
To get him some tripe;
But when she came back
He was smoking a pipe.

She went to the tavern
For white wine and red;
But when she came back
The dog stood on his head.

She went to the fruiterer's
To buy him some fruit;
But when she came back
He was playing the flute.

She went to the tailor's
To buy him a coat;
But when she came back
He was riding a goat.

She went to the hatter's
To buy him a hat;
But when she came back
He was feeding the cat.

She went to the barber's
To buy him a wig;
But when she came back
He was dancing a jig.

She went to the cobbler's
To buy him some shoes;
But when she came back
He was reading the news.

The Dame made a curtsey,
The dog made a bow;
The Dame said, "Your servant,"
The dog said, "Bow-wow."

## THE DOGS OF THE MONKS

The dogs of the monks
Of St. Bernard go,
To help little children
Out of the snow.
Each has a rum bottle
Under his chin,
Tied with a little bit
Of bobbin.

(Bobbin is narrow ribbon.)

## A RIDDLE

Two legs sat upon three legs
With one leg in his lap;
In comes four legs
And runs away with one leg;
Up jumps two legs,
Catches up three legs,
Throws it after four legs,
And makes him bring back one leg.

   (Two legs is a man; three legs is a
     stool; one leg is a leg of mutton;
     four legs is a dog.)

## THE DOGGIES WENT TO THE MILL

The doggies went to the mill,
This way and that way;
They took a lick out of this one's sack,
And they took a lick out of that one's sack,
And a leap in the stream, and a dip in the dam,
And went walloping, walloping, walloping
   HOME!

## THE LITTLE BLACK DOG

The little black dog ran round the house,
And set the bull a-roaring,
And drove the monkey in the boat,
Who set the oars a-rowing,
And scared the cock upon the rock,
Who cracked his throat with crowing.

## I HAD A LITTLE DOGGY

I had a little doggy that used to sit and beg;
But Doggy tumbled down the stairs and broke his little leg.
Oh! Doggy, I will nurse you, and try to make you well.
And you shall have a collar with a little silver bell.

## ROON, ROON, ROSIE

Roon, roon, rosie,
Cuppie, cuppie, shell,
The dog's away to Hamilton
To buy a new bell;
If you don't take it
I'll take it to myself.
Roon, roon, rosie,
Cuppie, cuppie, shell

## POOR DOG BRIGHT

Poor Dog Bright,
Ran off with all his might,
Because the Cat was after him,
Poor Dog Bright.

BUFF

I had a little dog, and they call'd him Buff;
I sent him to the shop for a hap'orth of snuff;
But he lost the bag, and spill'd the snuff,
So take that cuff, and that's enough.

## HEY DIDDLE, DIDDLE

Hey diddle, diddle,
The cat and the fiddle,
The cow jumped over the moon;
The little dog laughed
To see such sport,
And the dish ran away with
  the spoon.